Grott Street Gang

She called a meeting of the Grott Street
Gang that evening to make a new plan.

Three more *brilliant* Young Hippo School stories:

Off to School
Jean Chapman

Nightingale News
Odette Elliott

Class Four's Wild Week
Malcolm Yorke

Or dare you try a Young Hippo Spooky?

Ghost Dog
Eleanor Allen

The Screaming Demon Ghostie
Jean Chapman

The Green Hand
Tessa Krailing

Smoke Cat
Linda Newbery

The Kings' Castle
Ann Ruffell

Scarem's House
Malcolm Yorke

These Young Hippo Magic stories are fantastic!

My Friend's a Gris-Quok!
Malorie Blackman

Diggory and the Boa Conductor
The Little Pet Dragon
Philippa Gregory

Broomstick Services
Ann Jungman

The Marmalade Pony
Linda Newbery

Mr Wellington Boots
Ann Ruffell

The Wishing Horse
Malcolm Yorke

TERRY DEARY

The Grott Street Gang

Illustrated by Steve Donald

Scholastic Children's Books,
Commonwealth House,
1–19 New Oxford Street,
London WC1A 1NU, UK
a division of Scholastic Ltd
London ~ New York ~ Toronto ~ Sydney ~ Auckland
Mexico City ~ New Delhi ~ Hong Kong

First published by Scholastic Ltd, 1991
In this edition, 1996

Text copyright © Terry Deary, 1991
Cover illustration copyright © Steve Donald, 1996
Inside illustrations copyright © Steve Donald, 1991

ISBN 0 590 13732 8

Printed by Cox & Wyman Ltd, Reading, Berks.

10 9 8 7 6 5 4 3

Contents *.

DUCKPOOL CONSTABULARY

Absolutely confidential private top-secret report

SUBJECT:
The Grott Street Gang

As ruthless, truthless, toothless and useless a gang of villains as you could ever wish to meet!

Nancy Clogg —

Criminal mastermind — believed to be behind The Great School Dinner Disaster, at Duckpool Primary School.

WARNING!! Do not follow with sniffer dogs — one sniff of her socks will overpower them!

R.U. Watt —

Nancy Clogg's right-hand man — has a brain like Albert Einstein's — dead for nearly forty years.

WARNING!! Do not ask him any questions — he doesn't know the answers. He doesn't even know that two and two make five.

Ivan Dunno —

Nancy Clogg's left-hand man — has the brain of a cunning fox — but the fox wants it back.

WARNING!! Do not ask him any questions either. His dad is very big and can get a bit annoyed if Ivan is upset.

Egbert Hoo —

The gang's hit man —
when they get fed up
they hit him.

WARNING!! He bites! One teacher claims he bit the
ends off twenty pencils in one day.

Glen Snoddle —

The gang's getaway
driver — drives bikes,
drives skateboards
and drives teachers
round the bend.

WARNING!! He tells lies. Do not believe a word this
boy says — even if he is telling you the
truth.

Betty Ettrick —

The gang's goody-goody
— polite, well-behaved
and always does her
homework. She also does
Nancy's homework.

WARNING!! Nobody can be <u>that</u> good. Don't turn
your back on her or she might hit you
with her halo.

CONCLUSION: The Duckpool Constabulary have no
evidence whatsoever that the gang have ever done
anything wrong. But keep your eyes open and one day —
one lovely, lovely, lovely day — we might just catch them
at it. Then we'll really, <u>really</u> get them!

Signed:
    Police Constable

L. O. Elloe.

Chapter 1 - The Grott Street Gang

Nancy Clogg was not a nice girl.

Sorry. Nancy Clogg was a *nasty* girl.

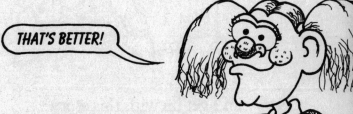

Nancy Clogg was the nastiest girl in Duckpool Primary.

Alright, Alright. Nancy Clogg was the nastiest girl in the whole world!

Now can I get on with this story?

Nancy was the leader of the Grott Street Gang—also known as the Famouser Five . . . don't ask me why.

'COS, STUPID, I ONCE READ A BOOK ABOUT THIS GANG CALLED THE FAMOUS FIVE. BORING LOADA KIDS WHO NEVER DID NOTHING EXCITING 'CEPT CATCH CROOKS. OUR GANG WAS GOING TO BE BETTER THAN THAT. FAMOUSER, IN FACT. SEE?

Thanks, Nancy. As I was saying, Nancy led the Grott Street Gang because she was the roughest, toughest, ugliest, scruffiest kid in the gang. She never washed behind her ears and changed her socks just once a week. But the main reason she was leader of the gang was because Nancy Clogg made the best plans.

IT'S TRUE.

Here is one of Nancy's plans, the five-a-side football plan:

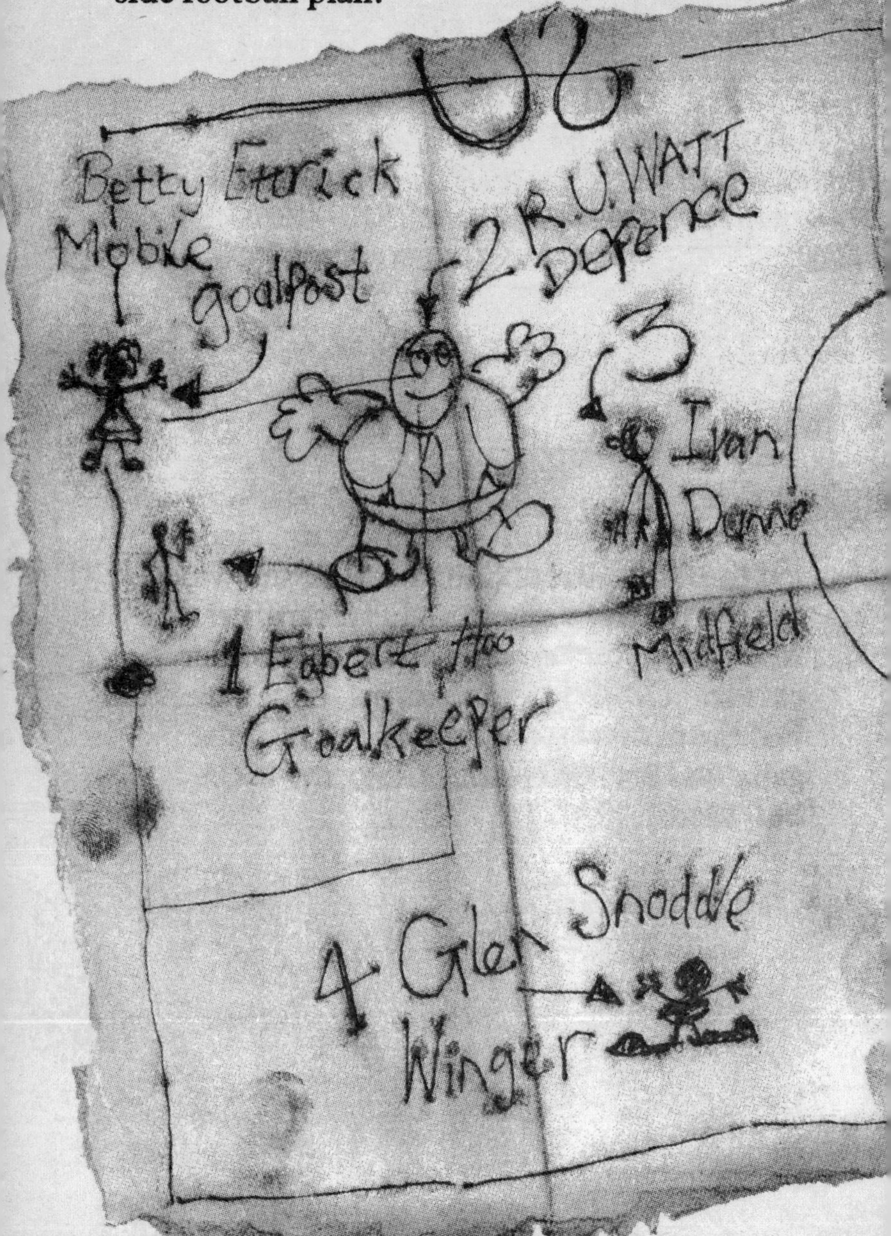

Betty Ettrick
Mobile
goalpost

2 R.U.WATT
Defence

3

Ivan
Dunne
Midfield

1 Egbert Hoo
Goalkeeper

4 Glen Snoddie
Winger

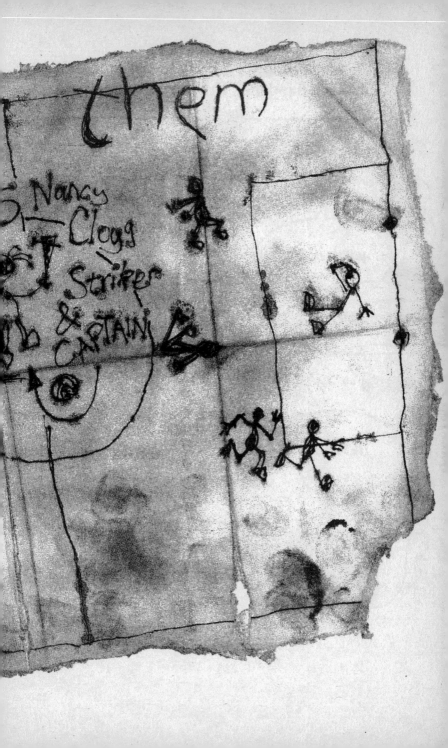

The team caused Nancy lots of problems.
Look what happened Friday morning . . .

You can see why it took about an hour to explain the team. Then Nancy had to explain the tactics . . .

It was. That was the cunning, cheating part of Nancy Clogg's plan. It was also the part that caused all the trouble with her class teacher, Miss Fitt.

The teams lined up on Friday lunchtime after a delicious school dinner of dog-food and chips.

STARTER

skunk
Soop   ·20p

MAIN course

Half
Stewed mince   ·20p

lumpy
Mashed Potato   ·20p

cold seaweed
Cabbidge   ·20p

AFTERS

Appul Pie and Custard ·20p

Indigestion Tablets £1·00

Please wash you're hands after
  eating you're dinner.

Some diners?
Smoking can damidge
          you're helth

The football match was a real needle match against Class 1 . . . The SSS . . . the Snotty-Spotty-Swats.

The SSS objected straight away.

The game began with the whistle.
(PEEEEEEEP!) Nancy passed to Glen
Snoddle . . . and Glen fell over the ball.

HE ALWAYS DOES.
I ONLY PICK HIM BECAUSE
THE BALL BELONGS TO HIM.

The ball ran to a SSS player—he ran for the
Grott Street Gang goal.

KICK HIM, DUNNO!

But Ivan Dunno was too busy picking his
nose to notice. The SSS had a clear shot at
goal! Egbert Hoo ran and hid in case he got
in the way of the shot. So that's when
Nancy's cheating plan came into effect.

Betty Ettrick, the moveable goal post, ran towards the other goal post so the goal was only two and a half centimetres wide. The SSS missed.

Nancy grabbed the SSS captain . . . but, just at that moment, Miss Fitt appeared on playground duty.

And Nancy saw her dreams of glory disappearing down the plug-hole.

THE MONDAY SPORT

CLOGG

Soccer super-star, Nancy Clogg, hit the old enemy SSS for six yesterday in a display of football ability that England manager, R o b b y B o b s o n , described as "out of this world". Not only did she score six magnificent goals but she overcame a broken leg to save a penalty.

Miss Clogg, still only ten years old, hopes to play for England one day – if she's not too busy being Miss World. Many top clubs, including Lanchester United, are after her signature – as soon as she can do joined-up writing she will give it to them.

Nancy is also manager

CLOUTS SIX PAST SSS

of Grott Street Gang Rovers, she invented the brilliant "moving goal post" tactic and washes the team strips by hand. After the game she described herself as "over the sun". The SSS captain said he was "sick as a zoo full of parrots".

As well as being awarded the "Person of the Match" trophy Nancy was given a one-hour detention by the evil Miss Fitt who is only jealous because Nancy is so good-looking.

And when those dreams of glory vanished
Nancy was upset.

Nancy never believed in holding a grudge.
Nancy believed in r–e–v–e–n–g–e!
REVENGE!
She called a meeting of the Grott Street
Gang that evening to make a new plan.

Chapter 2 - Getting Fitt

As the Grott Street Gang did Nancy's hundred sums that Friday lunchtime Nancy made her vengeful plans.

FATTY FITT HAS GONE TOO FAR THIS TIME. WE'RE GOING TO GET HER. LET HER TYRES DOWN!

The gang was not too keen. "Isn't it against the law to mess about with a teacher's bicycle?" Egbert Hoo asked.

"No," Nancy answered. "It's only against the law to get *caught* messing about with a teacher's bicycle!"

"And we won't get caught, Nancy?" Ivan asked as he wiped his nose on his sleeve . . . "Snnnnnnnt!"

I WISH HE WOULDN'T DO THAT. THAT'S WHAT SCHOOL TIES ARE FOR.

"We won't get caught because I will make one of my wonderful plans!" the leader told him. "First we decide what Miss Fitt likes!"

"Food!" young Betty Ettrick cried. "Fatty Fitt loves her food!"

"Starve her for a day or two!" R.U. Watt offered. "Tie a rope round her waist and dangle her over a cliff . . . like they did with smugglers in the old days."

"The nearest cliffs are fifty miles away!" Nancy scoffed.

"Well, chuck her off the school roof."

"And how do we get that big lummock on the roof in the first place?"

"Er . . . er . . ."

"And have you got a strong enough rope?"

"No, but I've got an incredible pair of braces!" R.U. said.

"Made of elastic, no doubt?"

"Yes, but very strong!"

"R.U. thick or R.U. Watt? Ha! Elastic! Imagine what would happen!"

"My dad could come and punch her nose," the short-legged Snoddle said.

"How big's your dad?"

"He's four foot six!"

"He couldn't even REACH her nose!"

Snoddle sniffed. "Well . . . he could punch her in the kneecaps!"

"Nah! Fitt's too fat to feel a fing . . .
I mean *thing*!" R.U. said.

"True. But an idea's running round in my
head," Nancy muttered.

"It has plenty of room to run in there!"
Snoddle sniggered. But Nancy wasn't
listening.

JUST AS WELL FOR HIM I WASN'T!

"Fitt's so fat . . . she wouldn't feel a
thing. Suppose we put a drawing pin on the
chair and she sat on it . . ." Nancy went on.

"She wouldn't feel it!" Egbert sniffled.
"She's too fat!"

"So she'd never know she'd been poisoned
till it was too late!" Nancy cried.

POISONED!!!!

"Yes, we'd put poison on the pin!" Nancy explained.

"Alright, Miss Smarty-pants," Snoddle sneered. "Where'd we get the poison? Didn't think of that, did you? Eh?"

The Grott Street Gang was silenced by the brilliance of Nancy's plan.

But the Grott Street Gang was still nervous. "What if you get caught, Nancy? Will you take the blame?" Egbert asked.

"I won't get caught because we're all in this together. Remember the motto, lads!"

"Er . . . no, actually, Nancy, we don't!" Dunno admitted.

"It's the same as the three Mustgetbeers . . .
one for all and all for one!" Nancy cried.
The Gang was quite excited by that.

So Nancy pinched the Ryd-ban poison—

GOOD NAME THAT; IT'LL RYD US OF MISS FITT AND BAN HER FROM OUR FOOTBALL GAMES!

—and dreamed the weekend away.

THE MONDAY EVENING GOSSIP

FOUL PLAY FEARED AS FITT FALLS FLAT ON FACE !!!!

"Big loss.": L. Canem – Head

Duckpool primary teacher, Miss Freda Fitt, was found lying flat on her face in the playground by a passing policeman. A hen and two chickens were seen running away so police suspect fowl play.

Was she pecked to pieces by these feathered fiends?

Or did she deliberately cause herself injury by sitting on a poisoned pin as police pathologist, Patrick Paine, pointed out to press reporters?

Bald

Bald headmaster, Mr Canem, said "Miss Fitt will not be returning to the school. She will be a big loss . . . a very big loss . . . a very, very big loss. We wi have great difficulty i finding someone to fi her shoes—, or he dress, for that matter."

Heroine

Local football heroine Nancy Clogg, said "Hee! hee! I'm ever so . . . ha! ha! ha! . . . sorry to lose her!"

Chapter 3 — The Poison Pin

The poison pin sat on Miss Fitt's chair.
All it needed now was for Miss Fitt to sit.

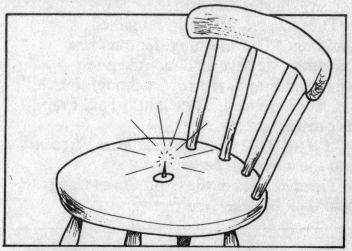

But Miss Fitt was late that Monday morning.

The Grott Street Gang had watched as Nancy dipped the pin in "Ryd-Ban" . . . and they had all crept into school early to make sure the pin was in place.

IT WAS THE FIRST TIME I'D EVER BEEN EARLY FOR SCHOOL IN MY LIFE!

At last Miss Fitt arrived.

"Good morning, Class 2!" she puffed.

"Good mor-ning, Miss Fi-itt!" Class 2 moaned back.

"Sit!" the teacher said.

The class sat. Miss Fitt remained standing. "This morning, for our class assembly, we have an honoured guest— Reverend Frapp, vicar of Duckpool church."

Class 2 groaned. They'd heard old Frapp-face drone on before.

"I'll just take the register," Miss Fitt said and she moved to her seat.

The members of the Grott Street Gang held their breaths . . .

Miss Fitt hovered . . . Miss Fitt lowered her
big body slowly . . .

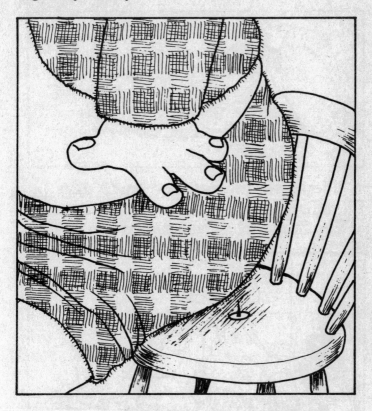

Then there was a knock on the door. The
door swung open and Reverend Frapp's
ferrety face peered round.

Miss Fitt pushed herself to her feet just in
time. "Good morning, Reverend," she
smiled.

Reverend Frapp entered the room. His nose curled as if at an unpleasant smell . . .

"Please take my seat, Reverend," Miss Fitt offered.

The Grott Street Gang gasped . . .

Reverend Frapp sat down . . .

Reverend Frapp jumped up . . .

Reverend Frapp screamed. He turned on Miss Fitt.

THAT WAS A MISTAKE!

THIS CLASS IS THE MOST ILL-MANNERED, UNTIDY AND INSOLENT GROUP OF CHILDREN I HAVE EVER COME ACROSS. THEY SHOULD ALL BE SEVERELY THRASHED AND GIVEN A GOOD, HOT BATH.

THAT DID IT.

Reverend Frapp slid out of the door like a slimy slug. The class went silent . . .

IT DID . . . YOU COULD HAVE HEARD A PIN DROP — A POISON PIN. MISS PICKED IT UP FROM THE FLOOR.

She sighed and said, "I suppose this was meant for me . . . well it wouldn't have worked anyway . . . my bum's too fat to feel it!" She grinned an evil grin. "Let me tell you something, class 2 . . . you may be wicked, but Mr Canem put me in charge of you lot for one very good reason . . . I'm *wickeder*!"

She licked her lips and smirked a cruel smirk. "For trying to stick a pin in me you'll do five hundred sums . . ."

WE GROANED.

"But Miss, it wasn't me!" the creepy Betty Ettrick cried.

Miss Fitt shrugged. "Until I find out who it was I'm going to make you all suffer . . . so tell me who it was, dear Betty?"

"The Grott Street Gang says, 'One for all and all for one'," Nancy cried. "You'll never get us to snitch!"

"That's right," young Betty sighed. "Sorry, Miss . . . I'd never tell you Nancy did it . . . even though she did!"

I GROANED. IF LOOKS COULD KILL THEN BETTY ETTRICK WOULD BE PUSHING UP DAISIES NOW!

"Thank you, Betty. Nancy Clogg has a thousand sums . . . the rest of you are free. In fact, for getting rid of that potty priest you'll get a treat. Next week I'll take you to the zoo!"

BUT DID NANCY CLOGG GET TO GO? NO CHANCE! LIKE MY DAD SAYS, "DON'T GET MAD, GET EVEN!" WHILE I DID DETENTION — AND THE FAMOUSER FIVE DID THE SUMS — I PLANNED MY GREATEST GET FITT PLAN EVER. LET ME TELL YOU ABOUT IT . . .

Just a moment! There's one thing I'm dying to know, Nancy. Why didn't the Reverend Frapp die of Ryd-Ban poisoning?

OH, I ASKED GRANDAD ABOUT THAT POISON. IT SEEMS GRAN WON'T LET HIM DRINK OR SMOKE IN THE HOUSE. SO HE SNEAKS DOWN TO THE GARDEN SHED WHERE HE HAS HIS LITTLE PLEASURES. HE HIDES THEM IN THE JARS AND MIXES UP THE LETTERS ON THE LABELS.

And "Ryd-Ban"?

WORK IT OUT . . . ALONG WITH ALL THE OTHERS IN HIS SHED.

And the Grott Street Gang's next cunning plan?

THE GREAT GORILLA GRAB! YOU MIGHT HAVE READ ABOUT IT IN THE PAPERS . . .

THE DUCKPOOL DAILY

GLADYS THE GORILLA GONE!

The gruesome Gladys, a grotesque gorilla, escaped from Duckpool Zoo. Lock your doors! Keep your cats in their

Ted Zed

N. Idiot

Gladys the Gorilla

kennels! Gladys is at large – very large – very, VERY large!

Zoo-keeper, Ted Zed said, "An idiot let her out!"

Mr N. Idiot of Duckpool High Street is reported as saying, "No I never!"

Miss Fitt

A party of children from Duckpool Primary were in the zoo at the time. Teacher, Miss Freda Fitt, said, "My children wouldn't do a thing like that. They'd sell you their granny for ten pence, they'd pinch a bun off a rabbit or fleece a sheep for five pence – they'd set fire to the school for free . . . but I have never known them to set a gorilla free. Why would they do that? Eh?"

Weedy pupil Egbert Hoo (9), said, "I saw a man do it. He was tall and thin with white hair."

The thief was also seen by R.U. Watt (9), who said, "Short black hair all the way down to his feet . . . he wasn't very tall, but he was as fat as Miss Fitt!"

Police are looking for a tall, fat, skinny dwarf with black and white hair. P.C. Cringle said, "If you see the suspect don't go near! Just offer it a banana and say, 'Who's a pretty girl, then?' "

56

Of course the Famouser Five had pinched Gladys. They agreed to say a tall thin man with white hair had taken him. I just don't understand why R.U. Watt gave another story . . .

BECAUSE HE'S THICK. WATTY HAD DESCRIBED THE **GORILLA!**

And while the gang was at the zoo Nancy was putting the finishing touches to her master plan at school. Miss Fitt had given Nancy the job of sticking 2F's pictures up on the classroom walls. She was using a can of spray-on wallpaper paste . . .

WHICH WAS EXACTLY WHAT I NEEDED FOR PART TWO OF THE GREAT GORILLA GRAB PLAN

Nancy met the gang the next morning.
Friday.

IT **HAD** TO BE FRIDAY. THAT WAS THE DAY FATTY
FITT ALWAYS HAD A BATH, YOU SEE?

No. I don't see. Never mind. It will all be
clear in time. The gang was excited.

GLADYS IS GREAT. CAN WE HAVE HER IN
THE GANG, NANCY?

YEH! SHE'LL MAKE A BETTER GOAL-
KEEPER THAN EGBERT! WITH THOSE
LONG ARMS!

Why did the gang need a gorilla and a fishing rod?

Nancy also pinched every door mat from the school. The gang spent morning break shaving the bristles off the mats. They collected them in a vacuum cleaner bag. And Gladys the gorilla?

HENRY! GET IN THE HOUSE AT ONCE! YOU NEED A SHAVE!

COUGH! GASP!

So Gladys was taken into the house and shaved by Granny. Granny was a little short-sighted, you understand.

MUCH BETTER, HENRY. I'VE NEVER SEEN YOU LOOK SO HANDSOME!

OOK!

GRANDAD HAD GONE TO THE PUB . . .

Everyone was happy. Nancy drew up her final plan.

I still don't understand what it's all about . . .

YOU'RE NOT SUPPOSED TO! IT'S SECRET. IF YOU WERE CLEVER LIKE ME THEN YOU'D BE ABLE TO WORK IT OUT, SEE!

Friday evening arrived. Miss Fitt set the class their homework . . . twenty spellings to be learned by Monday.

. . . AND LASTLY, THE WORD P–O–I–N–T–L–E–S–S.

MISS! WHAT DOES "POINTLESS" MEAN?

NEVER MIND WHAT IT MEANS — JUST LEARN HOW TO SPELL IT. STUPID GIRL.

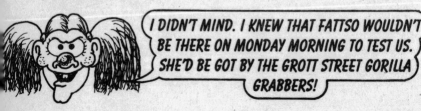

I DIDN'T MIND. I KNEW THAT FATTSO WOULDN'T BE THERE ON MONDAY MORNING TO TEST US. SHE'D BE GOT BY THE GROTT STREET GORILLA GRABBERS!

Chapter 5 - Gorillas and Glue

Night fell.

The Grott Street Gang gathered.

Nancy marched round to Betty's house . . . .

Mrs Ettrick answered the door and Nancy put on her sweetest smile.

LIKE THIS

PLEASE, MRS ETTRICK, CAN YOUR BETTY COME ROUND TO PLAY WITH MY DOLLIES?

BETTY! HERE'S THAT SMELLY GIRL TO SEE YOU. THE ONE WHO NEVER CHANGES HER SOCKS!

69

COME QUICKLY, BETTY. YOU'RE IN GREAT DANGER!

WHY, NANCY?

BECAUSE I'LL THUMP YOU IF YOU DON'T.

70

Now the gang was complete. The Famouser Five marched through the streets of Duckpool like the Magnificent Seven . . . except there were only six of them, of course.

They reached the house of the Fearsome Fitt. Bats hung by their toes from her telly aerial. Wolves howled in the wilderness at the bottom of her garden . . . at least that's what Nancy reckoned.

WELL, IT COULD HAVE BEEN NEXT DOOR'S DOG. IT WAS DARK, YOU KNOW!

Nancy sent Ivan Dunno into the dark back garden . . . he was the bravest.

While he was gone the gang checked their gear.

Nancy screamed.

74

Ivan Dunno reported back. He was short of breath.

NOT TO MENTION BRAINS.

SHE'S IN THE BATH! I CAN HEAR HER SPLASHING AN' HER RUBBER DUCK'S SQUEAKING!

RIGHT, DUNNO . . . TAP ON THE DOOR!

ER . . . THAT'S A FUNNY PLACE TO . . .

Ivan didn't finish. Nancy had her hands around his collar. That made it easy to rap on the door with the back of his head. Ouch!

Soon they heard the slap of Miss Fitt's feet on the hall floor.

The members of the Grott Street Gang leapt to their positions. What happened next was so fast Miss Fitt never knew what hit her.

Miss Fitt stood in the doorway — a towel wrapped around her dripping figure.

Glen Snoddle flicked his fishing rod and hooked the towel. He pulled. Miss Fitt was dragged out onto the front path . . .

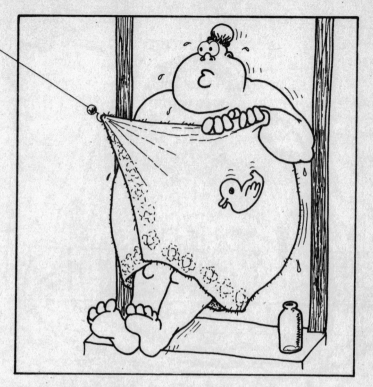

Snoddle pulled again. The towel flew off!

Yes, please!

Nancy called to Egbert Hoo . . .

Miss Fitt was locked out!

Now it was Nancy's turn to leap into action. She ran round Miss Fitt like a whirlwind and covered her with paste.

Then it was R. U. Watt's turn . . .

The boy took the bag of bristles and threw them over the teacher. The bristles stuck to the paste. Miss Fitt looked just like . . .

. . . a gorilla!

And now it was Betty Ettrick's turn.

Betty ran to the phone box on the corner. She dialled 9-9-9!

HELP! HELP! HELP! WE'VE FOUND GLADYS, THE ESCAPED GORILLA! COME AND GET HER AT ONCE!

Within a minute P.C. Cringle was there on his turbo-charged, twin-saddled bicycle. He had a rope round Miss Fitt in a trice.

Miss Fitt struggled and brought her mighty fist down on P.C. Cringle's helmet. That was a mistake. P.C. Cringle was armed. He pulled out his gorgonzola cheese sandwich and wafted it under Miss Fitt's nose.

OOCH! THAT WAS NASTY!

Freda Fitt didn't wake up till Monday morning in the zoo — and by then she was behind bars.

Ah, but it couldn't last, of course.

Well . . . er . . . what about when Miss Fitt
woke up? And when Granny found
Gladys . . . and when Mr Canem missed
Miss Fitt in the classroom?

I'D THOUGHT OF ALL THAT, OF COURSE!

WE MADE HEADLINE NEWS AGAIN! I ALWAYS KNEW I'D BE MORE FAMOUS THAN THE FAMOUS FIVE! FAMOUSER!

DUCKPOOL GAZETTE

GROTT STREET GANG GET GLADYS GORILLA!

Today Duckpool hails Nancy Clogg (10), and her gang, heroes. On Friday night they captured the awful ape, the gargantuan Gladys, Duckpool zoo's answer to King Kong.

Modest Nancy said. "It was nothing! It just took brains, courage, cunning and a fabulous leader. I'm the best footballer in the school too!"

Nancy Clogg – heroine

Zoo keeper Fred Zed (37) said, "Gladys is a litte worse for wear after her adventure. Seems a knock on her head has made her forget her name. She insists she's some teacher called Freda Fitt."

Fred Zed – zoo keeper

But the *Duckpool Gazette* called at Duckpool Primary to interview Nancy's heroes and met the charming Miss Fitt (29) there. Gladys must be mistaken.

Miss Fitt – charming

HM the Queen

The Queen sent a telegram to Nancy. It read: "Nice work, Nancy, finding that fiend; can you come to London some time, please? I've lost a corgi."

Nancy said she might go if the Queen will let her have a sit on the throne and a try on of her crown.

Ivan Dunno (9) said, "Nancy's head is probably now too big for it to fit." (Ivan is recovering in hospital after accidentally running into Nancy's right knee.)

Ivan Dunno – recovering

Mayor of Duckpool

The Mayor of Duckpool (96) said, "I'm proud of the lass! I've been to see this gorilla today! Fierce! It grabbed me by the throat and started screaming something about wallpaper paste and bristles. Mad as a box of cracker biscuits. Oh, by the way, can all gorillas talk?"

Lemmy Canem – Head

Nancy was offered a week's holiday by Headmaster Lemmy Canem (104), but she was keen to get back to her desk and her beloved teacher. *Duckpool Gazette* wishes all our youngsters were like Nancy Clogg!

But how did the Duckpool reporter see Miss
Fitt in the classroom when she was seen by
the mayor in the zoo at the same time?

EASY! IF MISS FITT TOOK GLADYS'S PLACE, THEN
WHY SHOULDN'T GLADYS TAKE MISS FITT'S
PLACE?

You mean you have a monkey for a teacher!

THAT'S RIGHT. GIVE HER A SHAVE EACH DAY,
STICK HER IN ONE OF GRAN'S DRESSES AND YOU
CAN'T TELL THE DIFFERENCE.

But she can't teach you!

NO. SHE JUST SITS THERE AND SAYS "OOK!" . . .
LIKE MOST TEACHERS, REALLY.

And what do you do?

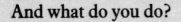

WE TEACH OURSELVES. LOTS OF FOOTBALL
LESSONS, OF COURSE . . . WE ALWAYS BEAT THE
SNOTTY-SPOTTY-SWATS THESE DAYS . . .

With Gladys in goal, I suppose.

'COURSE.

And where does Gladys
live?

GRANDAD'S SHED.

Doesn't Grandad mind?

'COURSE NOT. MEANS HE CAN SPEND EVERY
NIGHT DOWN AT THE PUB. GLADYS SPENDS THE
NIGHT WATCHING TELLY WITH GRANDMA,
EATING BANANAS.

94

A gorilla watches telly? Does she like it?

WELL, TARZAN'S HER FAVOURITE OF COURSE.

Come on, Nancy. You don't expect me to believe all this, do you?

BELIEVE IT? OF COURSE. TELL YOU WHAT. PUT IT IN SOME BOOK. LET THE KIDS OF MY AGE READ IT. THEY'LL BELIEVE IT. KIDS ARE BEST, YOU SEE . . . THEY KNOW THAT ANYTHING IS POSSIBLE IF YOU WANT TO BELIEVE IN IT. ISN'T THAT RIGHT, KIDS? TA-RA!